The Mekong River

Kim Dramer

Watts LIBRARY

Franklin Watts
A Division of Grolier Publishing
New York • London • Hong Kong • Sydney
Danbury, Connecticut

For George

Note to readers: Definitions for words in **bold** can be found in the Glossary at the back of this book.

Photographs ©: China Stock/Dennis Cox: 14, 16; Corbis-Bettmann: 40 (Leonard de Salva), 18, 19 (Lucia I. Tettoni), 28 (Michael S. Yamashita); Liaison Agency, Inc.: 48 (Wolfgang Käehler), 25 (Pasquier), 26 (Michael Yamashita), 2; Minden Pictures/Shin Yoshino: 15; Network Aspen: 31 (Jeffrey Aaronson), 23 (Radhika Chalasani); Photo Researchers: 32 (Alain Evrard), 33 (Georg Gerster), 50 (Stephenie Hollyman), 17 (Joyce Photographics), 29 (Noboru Komine), 20 (Alison Wright); Woodfin Camp & Associates: 5 bottom, 22, 46 (Geoffrey Clifford), 43 (Catherine Karnow), cover, 5 top, 8, 10, 12, 35, 36, 38, 45, 49 (Michael Yamashita).

Map by Bob Italiano

Visit Franklin Watts on the Internet at:
http://publishing.grolier.com

Library of Congress Cataloging-in-Publication Data

Kim Dramer
  The Mekong River / by Kim Dramer.
    p. cm.— (Watts library)
  Includes bibliographical references and index.
    ISBN 0-531-11854-1 (lib. bdg.)   0-531-13985-9 (pbk.)
    1. Mekong River—Juvenile literature. 2. Mekong River Valley—Description and travel—Juvenile literature. [1. Mekong River] I. Title. II. Series.
DS522.6 .D73 2001
959.7—dc21

00-031918

Contents

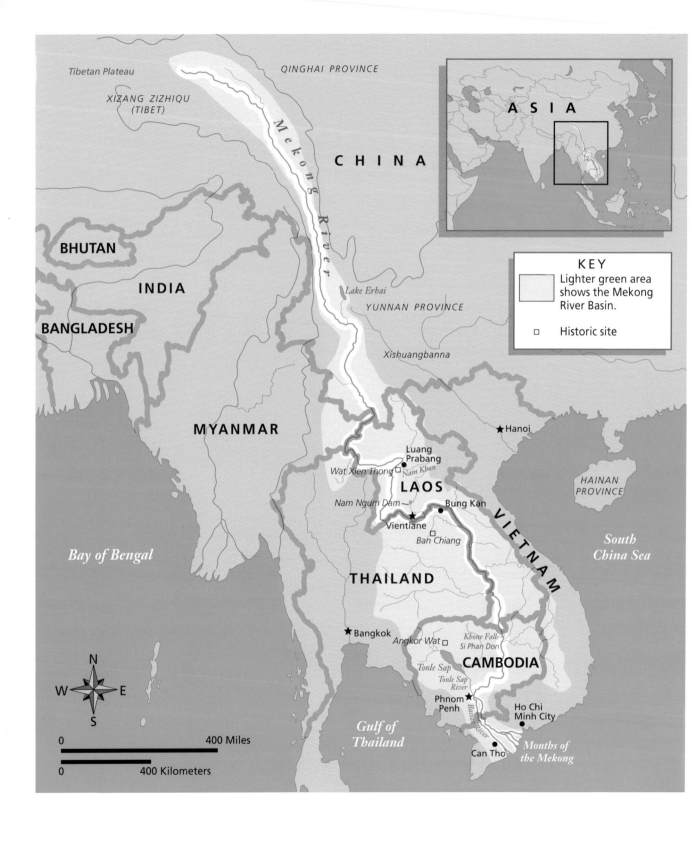

Tibetan Plateau

QINGHAI PROVINCE

XIZANG ZIZHIQU
(TIBET)

ASIA

CHINA

Mekong River

BHUTAN

INDIA

Lake Erhai

YUNNAN PROVINCE

BANGLADESH

Xishuangbanna

KEY

Lighter green area
shows the Mekong
River Basin.

□   Historic site

MYANMAR

Hanoi

Luang
Prabang

Wat Xien Thong   □   Nam Khan

LAOS

HAINAN
PROVINCE

Nam Ngum Dam

Bung Kan

Vientiane

VIETNAM

South
China Sea

Ban Chiang

Bay of Bengal

THAILAND

Bangkok

Khone Falls

Angkor Wat   □   Si Phan Don

Tonle Sap

CAMBODIA

Tonle Sap
River

Phnom
Penh

Ho Chi
Minh City

Bassac River

N
W   E
S

Gulf of
Thailand

Can Tho

Mouths of
the Mekong

0   400 Miles

0   400 Kilometers

Chapter One

Mother of Rivers

The Mekong River begins in the snow-covered mountains of the Tibetan Plateau, a high, flat raised area that is often called "the Roof of the World." The melted snow gathers force as it cuts through steep mountain gorges in south-west China. The river travels 2,600 miles (4,180 kilometers) across Asia, from its **source** in the Tibetan Plateau to its **mouths** in the South China Sea.

Over the centuries, the rushing waters of the river have cut gorges through the earth as deep as the Grand Canyon. Whitewater, rapids, and whirlpools characterize the currents of the river in China. Its fierce waters race across China to the southwestern part of Yunnan Province.

The Mekong crosses China's border and flows into Southeast Asia in the area known as the **Golden Triangle**. Here, where the borders of Myanmar (formerly known as Burma), Laos, and Thailand meet, the river changes character. The Mekong flows gently east and south through Laos to the **Khone Falls**. Then, in a mighty rush, the rapids cut through Cambodia (now Kampuchea) to arrive at the capital city of

The waters of the Mekong race through the Khone Falls.

A River With Many Names

The changing nature of the Mekong has resulted in different names for the river. At its rushing headwaters, Tibetans call the river *Dza Chu*, meaning "Water of Stone." The roaring waters that cut through China in a frenzy of whirlpools and whitewater are called *Lancang Jiang*, meaning "Turbulent River."

Below China, in Southeast Asia, the waters of the lower Mekong River Basin change character. Here, the Cambodians call the river *Tonle Thom*, which means "Great Water." In Thailand and Laos, the life-giving river is called *Mae Nam Khong* or *Mènam Khong*, meaning "Mother of Rivers." The English name for the river Mekong comes from these names. The Vietnamese name *Cuu Long*, or Nine Dragons, describes the branching of the river as it flows to empty in the South China Sea.

Phnom Penh. With a population of nearly one million people, Phnom Penh is the largest city along the Mekong.

The river meanders lazily through the landscape of Southeast Asia. The waters branch into two rivers, the Bassac and the Mekong, while from the north the *Tonle Sap* (Great Lake) River joins them. The French who colonized Cambodia in the 1800s called this **confluence** Quatre Bras, which means "Four Arms."

The Bassac and the Mekong flow south side by side to Vietnam. In Vietnam, the Mekong sprawls out before reaching the South China Sea. The Vietnamese compare the river to a great dragon with a head that roars and foams in the mountains and a tail that swishes restlessly in the **delta**, a network of streams and channels.

Life on the Lower Mekong

The Lower Mekong, from the Golden Triangle to the South China Sea, is the longest river in Southeast Asia. This stretch of the river, some 1,000 miles (1,600 km), is the only part of

Most Vietnamese people use a traditional, flat-bottomed boat called a sampan to travel the Mekong.

the vast waters of the Mekong River that is deep enough and wide enough for ships to travel.

The waters of the Lower Mekong River Basin are a life-giving source to the people who live along its banks. They grow rice with waters from the Mekong and fish in its rich waters. Boats crowd the river, carrying people engaged in travel and trade. Here in Southeast Asia, the floods and tides of the Mekong River form the rhythm of life. In the tropical climate, the lazy waters of the Mekong rise and fall along with two annual monsoons. The depth and character of the Mekong change dramatically during each season.

The relationship between the river and the people who have lived by its banks dates back to prehistoric times. Over the centuries, people along the Mekong have continually adapted to the changing waters of the river. Changes in weather, wars and political upheavals, pollution and progress have all made their mark on the waters of the Mekong. And each year, people who farm, fish, travel, and trade along the river adapt to the changes. As a result, the Mekong—the Mother of Rivers—continues to sustain their lives.

Changing Winds

A **monsoon** is a seasonal wind that changes direction every six months. During the summer, the monsoon brings moist winds from the ocean. Heavy rains then flood the lands for rice farming. In winter, dry winds blow from the land to the sea.

At its upper reaches, people cross the Mekong using rope bridges.

Chapter Two

People and the Mekong

Almost half of the Mekong River runs through China, but there are few signs of human life as it passes through the rough terrain of Qinghai Province and Tibet in western China. The only structures that cross the fierce Mekong waters here are traditional rope bridges. One at a time, people cross deep gorges on these rope bridges.

Reaching China's southwestern Yunnan Province, the river flows through remote, hard to reach mountains. Here,

This temple sits on Putuo Island in Lake Erhai.

the land becomes filled with towering peaks and deep valleys. Following the river through Yunnan, the population is sparse, but nowhere along its entire length does the Mekong present a greater variety of ethnic groups. Each group of people has its own dress, language, and customs.

Lake *Erhai* (Ear Lake)—named for its shape—feeds water into the Mekong. This area supports twenty-four of China's ethnic minorities. The people follow a traditional way of life, growing crops on fields carved out of the hillsides. To supplement their farm crops, people hunt for food with traditional crossbows.

The Xishuangbanna district in the far south of Yunnan Province is the final stretch of the Mekong in China. The name comes from the local dialect, *dai sip song bana*, meaning "twelve administrative units." Jinghong, the provincial capital

Animals of the Mekong

Native species of the Xishuangbanna region include wild elephants, rhinoceroses, tigers, monkeys, and crocodiles.

of Xishuangbanna district, is the first large riverside town along the Mekong.

In Xishuangbanna, scores of tributaries run off the Mekong, breaking up the land between the hills into lush valleys and plains. The river basin area is a subtropical environment that has a staggering variety of plants and animals. The region is especially famous for its exotic butterflies and birds.

The Dai

The Dai people, whose legendary origins link them to the waters of the Mekong, are the largest ethnic group in the region. Long ago, according to a Dai story, hunters giving

chase to a golden deer found an earthly paradise. Settling in this land, they prospered until the arrival of a demon. A young Dai chased the demon, which fled to the river. The two struggled beneath the waters until the Dai emerged victorious, holding a magic pearl he had pulled from the demon's throat.

For more than one thousand years, the Dai have celebrated their New Year in mid-April with the Water Splashing Ceremony. No one escapes a drenching in the waters, which are said to wash away the dirt, sorrows, and demons of the past year and bring the happiness of the new year. During the three-day festival, people flock to the Mekong to compete in boat races, which celebrate yet another legend linking the Dai with the Mekong.

This story tells how two young men competed for the hand of a young Dai girl by having a boat race. One of them—a simple hunter—was the girl's true love, but the girl's father favored the other suitor, a prince. The Mekong, sensing the love the two young people had for one another, swamped the prince's boat with a huge wave. The hunter and the maiden were married after the victory.

Today, forty to sixty rowers paddle canoes of great length in New Year boat races. Gong players and drummers keep time for the rowers. One person sits in the prow, or front, of each boat, and rocks the boat to sway the hull and thus gain an advantage on the Mekong's waters.

The Golden Triangle

Leaving China, the Mekong begins its journey through Southeast Asia. Here, it is the area's longest river. The Mekong now flows through the area known as the Golden Triangle, where the countries of Myanmar, Laos, and Thailand meet. These countries have no control over the outlying mountain areas in the Golden Triangle, an area known for growing poppies used to make the drugs opium and heroin. Poppies are an important part of the area's economy, which is controlled by local groups and rebel movements with private armies.

The growers take sap from the poppy flowers and make it into opium. At least two-thirds of the world's opium supply comes from here. Recently, the United Nations has been

People make drugs from poppies, such as those shown here.

trying to eliminate the poppy farming and drug production in the area by introducing alternative cash crops, such as coffee and tobacco.

In this part of Southeast Asia, countries are divided by mountains, but they are connected and defined by rivers. The Mekong and its tributaries have always been routes for communication, travel, and trade. These waterways allow people to ship goods and share cultures. The Mekong River forms links between the peoples who live in the lower Mekong River Basin as well as those who live on the borders between Myanmar and Laos and between Laos and Thailand.

Today, nearly one in every three people in Cambodia (Kampuchea), Laos, Thailand, and Vietnam live in the lower Mekong River Basin. Most of these people are farmers. Over the centuries, traditional rice farming in the lower Mekong Basin has linked the people, the land, and the Mekong.

Early Peoples of the Mekong

The lower Mekong is rich in history. Archaeological excavations have found a number of prehistoric sites along the river. Some of the earliest agriculture and metalworking in human history may have taken place here.

At Ban Chiang in Thailand, excavations have uncovered evidence of a tranquil farming and hunting people who lived along the Mekong from 4 B.C. to A.D. 200. The ancient people of Ban Chiang built thatched huts on pilings. They tamed and raised cattle, pigs, chickens, and dogs, and grew rice.

In Ban Chiang, a museum displays archaeologists' discoveries.

This photo shows the Mekong during the summer southwestern monsoon season.

Chapter Three

Source of Life

The Mekong River, with its annual rising and receding floods, establishes the rhythm of life for the people and animals in the lower Mekong River Basin. The water levels drop during the winter northeast monsoon, and six months later, the river floods its banks during the summer southwestern monsoon. The people who live along the river, as well as the plant and animal life, have learned to adapt to the Mekong's seasonal changes.

A group of workers harvests rice.

Farming by the Mekong

The layers of silt carried by the river during the seasonal floods create rich soil for farmers along the Mekong Valley. The most important food source nourished by the waters of the Mekong is rice, the staple food of Southeast Asia. The Mekong River Basin is known as the rice basket of Southeast Asia. After the United States, Thailand and Vietnam are the world's leading exporters of rice.

People of the River

There is a saying in Southeast Asia that the Lao people live near the water, the Cambodians live on it, and the Vietnamese live in it. This describes the variety of lifestyles of the people along the Mekong River. For the Lao, the Mekong travels the entire length of their country. The Cambodians build houses on stilts to live above the Mekong waters during monsoon season. And many Vietnamese in the south live on boats in the Mekong.

Today, more than four hundred varieties of rice are available for cultivation. Each farmer's choice depends upon the quality and character of soil and the Mekong water in the fields. In summer, the swollen river flows into streams and canals as well as small lakes and reservoirs until the lands are flooded. The highest water levels are reached when the wet southwest monsoons blow from July to October. The waters of the Mekong carry a heavy load of river silt that is deposited along its banks. Rice thrives in these nourishing floodwaters. Other crops such as groundnuts, sesame, cotton, soybeans, and corn are also grown on the banks of the Mekong.

The northeast monsoon winds that blow from November to May bring the dry season and low levels of water. During the dry season, farmers dig ditches around rice fields and stock them with fish which they raise and feed. In the rainy season when the fields are underwater, the fish swim to the fields and find food. The fish fertilize the soil with their droppings and protect the rice by eating insects and weeds.

Water buffalo are used to plow the fields in traditional rice farming along the Mekong. The buffalo graze on rice stubble left after the

A farmer plows a rice field in Vietnam.

**Farming
Traditions**

Traditionally, men
work at plowing and
irrigation. Women
transplant and weed
the rice crop.

harvest. Rice straw is used to cover young plants to keep in moisture, and the ashes of burned straw are used to fertilize the fields. In this way, all the elements of life on the river are linked to one another, forming an ideal ecological pattern of growth, death, and regeneration, year after year.

Life in the Basin

The lower Mekong Basin waters provide a rich environment for marine life. Helped by a variety of plants, a warm climate, and abundant monsoon rains, the waters of the Mekong serve as fish spawning and nursery areas for hundreds of species of fish.

The summer flooding, brought by heavy, rain-bearing clouds and the melting snows of the Tibetan Plateau, releases nutrients from the soil. It helps vegetation to decompose and aquatic plants and algae to multiply. The waters of the Mekong push inland, flooding the land. The floodwaters of the Mekong create rapids that churn oxygen into the water and break up plants. Rocks offer shelter for insects, snails, and algae. All these events provide food and favorable conditions for spawning for the fish of the Mekong River.

During the summer, the heavy waters spill over the river-banks and flood the forests that line the banks of the Mekong. The fish invade the forests, searching for places to spawn and feeding on decomposing leaves and branches. Ecologists often describe the Mekong floodwaters as a "great soup of vegetation and fish."

The numerous fish species found in the waters of the Mekong include featherback, carp, catfish, swamp eel, snakehead, mackerel, spring eel, herring, needlefish, and anchovy. Regional fishermen use a variety of tools for each different type of fish: harpoons, throw nets, dragnets, lines, and hooks as well as fish traps made of bamboo and rattan. Sharks and dolphins are also found in these waters.

Fish traditionally make up half of the animal protein diet of people living in the lower Mekong Basin. Every meal consists of rice, seafood, and plant life all nourished by the Mekong's waters. People gather shrimp, crabs, snails, clams, mussels, frogs, and snakes from the river and its surrounding wetlands. They also harvest algae and other edible plants from its banks.

A woman gathers a basket full of shellfish in the Mekong Delta.

The newly independent countries of Southeast Asia sought more productive ways to raise food crops than traditional farming.

Chapter Four

Independent Mekong

After World War II (1939–1941), the countries of Southeast Asia regained their independence when the European colonialists withdrew. In the 1950s, Laos, Thailand, Cambodia (Kampuchea), and Vietnam wanted to increase their own resources, such as food and electricity, to become more modern and industrial nations. As always, these countries turned to the waters of the Mekong River to find solutions.

Mekong Development Committee

In 1957, the governments of Laos, Thailand, Cambodia, and Vietnam formed the Committee for Coordination of Investigations in the lower Mekong Basin. The organization was founded with the guidance and support of the United Nations. In the 1990s, China and Myanmar (Burma) joined the committee's efforts and discussions. The members of the **Mekong Development Committee** sought ways to work together. They wanted to "promote, coordinate, supervise, and control the planning and investigation of water resources development projects in the lower Mekong Basin."

This photo shows a dam across the Mekong River under construction in China.

The committee thought the traditional Mekong farming patterns, which relied on the annual monsoons, were obstacles to using more modern and productive farming methods. The new goal was to provide constant irrigation by creating reservoirs behind large dams. It was believed that these dams would also provide cheap electricity to the region and allow for industrialization of the new nations.

The members of the Mekong Development Committee decided to build a series of dams designed as great plugs for the waters of the Mekong.

28

Rain from the rainy season would then be stored in reservoirs and used for large-scale irrigation and **hydroelectric energy**. The irrigation projects along the Mekong were given top governmental priority.

Troubles for the Mekong

While the Mekong Development Committee hoped that the dams and irrigation projects would help people in the area, these efforts had some disastrous side effects. The chemical fertilizers, pesticides, and the machinery used in the project created ecological problems for the Mekong River and its

Many farmers had problems with their farms because of the dams and irrigation projects.

Opposite: In Laos, people rely on the Mekong River for farming and travel.

farmers. The chemicals polluted the waters and rice field tractors destroyed the frogs and worms that kept pests away from the crops.

Damming the waters of the Mekong caused more problems. The dams cut off the flow of vital silt and nutrients downstream to fisheries and rice fields, and prevented the fish from migrating. Upstream, dams drowned farmland along the Mekong and its tributaries. Farming populations that had lived along the banks of the Mekong for generations were relocated to higher lands unsuitable for farming.

At present, people along the banks of the Mekong River are among the poorest in the world. Past efforts have concentrated on technical changes, missing important human and ecological needs. The dams of the 1950s solved some problems but created others. Populations had to be relocated and wildlife habitats and fish migration were damaged or lost. The hope is that the "Mother of all Waters" will once again support and nourish the lives of all the people who live along this great river.

Today, people realize technological change must make allowances for environmental and social factors. As always, the Mekong River remains a river of hope, holding the promise of recovery for those whose lives are linked with its waters.

Chapter Five

Laos

The blue stripe in the center of the flag of Laos represents the waters of the Mekong and the river's central importance to the country's economy, history, and culture. Most of the country's cities can be found on or near the Mekong. The Mekong River travels the entire length of Laos, flowing down from China and into Cambodia. From this point on, the Mekong travels through land that was French **Indochina**. Laos, Vietnam, and Cambodia were protectorates under the control and protection of France in the late 1800s.

Mekong Highway

Dense forests cover Laos, making travel over land difficult. People use the Mekong and its tributaries, making these waterways the country's true highways.

Ancient and Modern Cities

Luang Prabang, the old royal residence of Laotian kings, and Vientiane, the capital city of today's Laos, are both located on the Mekong River. Luang Prabang, located at the confluence of the Mekong River and the Nam Khan, is home to *Haw Kham* (the Royal Palace Museum) that houses Buddhist royal religious objects. The museum displays a solid-gold standing Buddha weighing more than 100 pounds (45 kilograms). Elephant tusks engraved with Buddhas and silk embroidered by Laotian queens are also on exhibit.

At the northern tip of the peninsula formed by the Mekong and the Nam Khan is the *Wat Xien Thong* (Gold City Temple) built in 1560. The temple is now a funeral chapel with urns holding the ashes of the royal family. Across the Mekong River

The Wat Xien Thong is located in Luang Prabang.

the waters have carved out caves in the soft limestone. Here is the *Wat Long Khun*, a temple where the kings of Laos spent three days in retreat before they were crowned.

Vientiane is both the largest city in Laos as well as the country's capital. The *Pha That Luang*, or Great Sacred Stupa, symbolizes both the sovereignty of Laos and its Buddhist religion. Laotians believe that a breastbone of the Buddha was enshrined here in the third century B.C. The Great Sacred Stupa is designed to be climbed by the faithful so that at each

A monk departs the Pha That Luang, or Great Sacred Stupa.

of its levels, Buddhist teachings are encountered and considered. Each November, hundreds of monks assemble here for the *That Luang* Festival, a weeklong celebration.

Under French Rule

During colonial rule, the French undertook a series of explorations up the Mekong River. They were looking for a waterway to China. They wanted to ship tea and silks from China down the Mekong River to their ports in Indochina for export to Europe. In the mid-1800s, six groups of explorers started the journey, but none could get past the Khone Falls.

Along with exploring the region, the French tapped the area's natural resources, especially the precious woods, such as teak. The French colonial rulers began harvesting the logs during the 1800s. They used elephants to haul the logs from the forest to the Mekong for shipment to Europe.

European Explorers

In the past, it was believed that the Mekong and other rivers of Southeast Asia all originated in a huge lake in China. In 1866, Ernest-Marc-Louis Doudart de Lagrée led a French expedition that traveled up the Mekong River to southwestern China. They endured terrible hardships and frequent illnesses. Doudart de Lagrée died in 1868, three months before the end of the journey. His second in command, Francis Garnier, took charge of the exploration after his death. By June 1868, the expedition had mapped 4,000 miles (6,430 km) of land that had not previously been surveyed. But they failed to find the legendary origins of the Mekong.

After achieving independence from France in 1953, Laos earned more than one-third of its export income from logging. Unfortunately, the heavy logging caused erosion on mountainsides. The resulting silting of the Mekong has clogged the river's reservoirs.

Khone Falls

Called the Spirit Trap (*Leepee*) by the Laotians, the Khone Falls is not a single majestic fall such as the Niagara Falls. It is made up of a series of interlocking falls and cascades some 7 miles (11 km) long, spanning the entire width of the Mekong. At the Khone Falls, the Mekong is 6 miles (10 km) wide and 98 feet (30 m) deep.

Above the falls, the Mekong splits into many swiftly flowing streams encircling small islands. This area is called *Si Phan Don* (Four Thousand Islands). During the rainy season, this is the widest part of the Mekong, but the waters recede during the dry season. Thousands of islands, large and small, are uncovered in a 31-mile (50-km) stretch. The varied habitats and conditions of the Mekong at Si Phan Don form the richest

A person catches fish with a net in the rough waters of the Khone Falls.

35

fishing grounds of the Mekong. The area is home to the crown jewel of the Mekong—the Irawaddy dolphin. The Laotians believe that dolphins help fishermen to bring in huge catches, and save people from drowning.

The Nam Ngum Dam

The Nam Ngum Dam on the Mekong, about 56 miles (90 km) north of Vientiane, was designed to produce energy for the capital city and extra electricity to sell to Thailand. A huge artificial lake was created, and many Laotian farmers were

This photo shows one of the forests destroyed by the creation of the Nam Ngum Lake.

relocated. This project was started in 1971 by the Mekong Development Committee and sponsored by the World Bank.

The dam project destroyed additional forests and drowned large numbers of animals. The rotting vegetation from the forests led to a dip in oxygen that killed many fish. The lake then became a breeding ground for parasites and mosquitoes carrying deadly diseases such as malaria, dengue fever, and lung fluke.

In addition, the Laotians were traditional river fishermen and ill equipped for deep-lake fishing. The trunks of trees drowned by the dam damaged their nets. Their traditional way of life, dependent on the bounty of the Mekong River, was destroyed.

Yet, the waters of the Mekong continue to define Laotian culture. A pre-Buddhist rain festival, *Bun Bang Fi* (Rocket Festival), is still celebrated each May to coincide with the monsoon. Bamboo rockets are shot into the sky to prompt the heavens to send water to the rice fields. In July, *Khao Phansaa*, or Buddhist "Rains Retreat," begins. Buddhist monks retreat to a single monastery where they remain for three months so as not to damage young rice plants during their wandering.

Bun Nam (The Water Festival) marks the end of the rains and the swift fall of the river's level. The people then compete in **pirogue** races on the Mekong. These boats are carved out of a single tree trunk up to 90 feet (27 m) long and are manned by up to 60 paddlers.

New Year

In mid-April, the Laotians celebrate *Pii mai*, or the lunar year. As part of the holiday, the waters of the Mekong are used to clean houses and wash images of Buddha. Later, people throw water on one another in the streets

The Tonle Sap River meets the Mekong near Phnom Penh, the capital of Cambodia.

Chapter Six

Cambodia

The Tonle Sap River connects the Mekong with the Tonle Sap, or Great Lake, of Cambodia. It is the only known waterway in the world that flows in opposite directions at different times of the year. Under the light of the full moon each November, the king of Cambodia calls on the waters of the Tonle Sap to change their course and flow into the Mekong.

This ceremony coincides with the seasonal monsoons and the pull of the moon on the waters. As the waters of the Tonle Sap flow back into the Mekong River, the Great Lake subsides. Fish and

fingerlings move into the river and the waters fill with fish, which Cambodians rush to harvest. When the summer monsoons and melting snows of the Tibetan Plateau swell the waters of the Mekong, the Tonle Sap changes direction. It then drains into the Great Lake, causing it to become four times larger in size to 3,861 square miles (10,000 sq. km).

The Lost Capital

Northeast of the Tonle Sap, dense forests and jungles dominate the vast basin in Cambodia's interior. In the 1800s, European colonial powers rediscovered **Angkor**, the lost capital of the ancient **Khmer** empire in this dense jungle.

This group of explorers visited Angkor Wat in 1868.

Europeans who first saw the city compared it to the lost temple of King Solomon.

The name *Angkor* means "city" in Sanskrit, the classic language of India and Hinduism. Angkor has both Hindu and Buddhist temples. The teaching of these religions reached the ancient Khmer via traders and teachers traveling between India and China. Angkor was the Khmer empire's capital city as well as its religious center. The walled city was called *Angkor Thom*, or "Great City," and its most famous temple was *Angkor Wat* (Temple of Angkor).

The Khmer kings spent more than four hundred years constructing different temples at Angkor. These were dedicated to Hindu and Buddhist gods and to their kings, whom they regarded as earthly forms of the gods themselves. The Khmer king was a god-ruler or devi-raj. Angkor was conceived as a heaven on Earth, with Mount Merlu, the home of the gods, standing as a great tower at its center. This temple-mountain became the funerary monument for the god-ruler upon his death. The magnificence of Angkor's buildings is paired with a remarkable water-control system. This system was made up of irrigation canals and water storage tanks that regulated the waters of the Tonle Sap and Great Lake via reservoirs called *barays*.

Sandstone was quarried and sent by raft through the jungle. The waters of Mekong tributaries were used in the moats to represent the oceans that surrounded the temples and towers that were used to represent mountains. These moats were

Religions of Angkor

Buddhism is a religion based on the teachings of an Indian prince named Siddhartha Gautama, who lived during the fifth century B.C. He is also known as Buddha, which means "the enlightened one." Hinduism is based in part on ancient scriptures called the Veda.

also used for rituals, defense, irrigation, drainage, transportation, fish and waterfowl breeding, bathing, and drinking.

Ironically, the very structures meant to strengthen the power of the god-rulers brought an end to their rule. The cost of building Angkor Wat had greatly weakened the Khmer kingdom. In 1172, **Champa** armies sailed up the Mekong, crossed the Tonle Sap and burned the capital to the ground.

Jayavarman VII

The Khmer had to wait for the emergence of a new god-ruler to rebuild Angkor. This was Jayavarman VII (1182–1201), a Buddhist king. He defeated the Champa in land and naval battles fought on the lakes and canals. He then pursued the invaders into their own territory and seized their lands.

Jayavarman VII then constructed Buddhist monuments at Angkor, which he rebuilt and made his capital. Under his rule, Angkor Thom had one million inhabitants, more than any European city of the time. At Angkor, he constructed the large temple called the **Bayon** dedicated to Buddha.

Jayavarman VII was the last of the god-rulers to build at Angkor. The Mongols under Kublai Khan pushed the borders of the Chinese empire south, driving the Annamites of northern Vietnam, the Champa of southern Vietnam, and the Thai before them. The Thai eventually conquered the Khmer empire. The jungle became the final conqueror of Angkor. Its green veil hid the glories of Angkor for centuries.

Angkor

The city of Angkor and its temples cover 156 square miles (404 sq. km), an area roughly the size of Manhattan Island. It is the largest religious site in the world.

Political Turmoil

From 1975 to 1979, the **Khmer Rouge**, under the leadership of Pol Pot, tried to break Cambodia's modern history of monarchy, colonialism, and Western imperialism. Pol Pot dreamed of re-creating the agriculturally based Khmer empire. Instead, he created the infamous "killing fields." Thousands of Cambodians, whose only crimes were having contact with the West or being educated, were treated brutally and executed. After the expulsion of the Khmer Rouge from the area, it was found that only one Cambodian archaeologist who worked at Angkor had survived the killing fields. But the Khmer Rouge had not, as feared, destroyed the site.

The new government could do little to prevent the looting of Angkor. Cambodian peasants, desperate to rebuild their lives, stole carved stones and sold them to Western collectors. Since 1992, however, Angkor has been a World Heritage site, receiving guidance and support from the United Nations Educational, Scientific, and Cultural Organization (UNESCO). With UNESCO, special programs have been established to help protect Angkor.

Phnom Penh

Phnom Penh, the largest city on the Mekong River, has been the capital of Cambodia since the mid-1400s. It stands at the point the French named *Quatre Bras*, meaning "Four Arms." Here, the Mekong curves broadly, forming one side of an "X." The other half of the letter is formed by the junction of the Tonle Sap and the Bassac tributary.

Silver Pagoda

The floor of the Silver Pagoda in Phnom Penh is covered with more than 5,000 silver tiles. The pagoda houses a life-sized statue of Buddha made from 198 pounds (90 kilograms) of gold and decorated with 9,584 diamonds. The largest of these diamonds weighs 25 carats.

Cambodian legends tell of four statues of the Buddha that floated down the waters of the Mekong during the 1300s. The Mekong current deposited the Buddhas on a hill at the meeting of the Mekong, the Bassac, and the Tonle Sap rivers. The statues were discovered by a woman named Penh and a temple was built on the hill to house the statues. Phnom Penh means the "Hill of Penh."

Close to one million people live in the city of Phnom Penh, according a 1994 estimate.

A fishing boat navigates the Mekong in Vietnam.

Chapter Seven

Vietnam

The mouths of the Mekong River are found in southern Vietnam where its waters empty into the South China Sea. Shortly after crossing the Cambodian border into southern Vietnam, the Bassac and the Mekong Rivers begin to twist and turn. The Vietnamese call the Mekong the *Tien* (Upper River). The Bassac is called the *Han* (Lower River).

The fast-moving waters of the Bassac and Mekong pick up soil and sand and carry them downstream toward the mouths of the river. The soil and sand carried in its water are deposited on the river bottom.

As the deposits get bigger, they block the river's mouth. The river splits again and again to find a new path to the sea. A network of streams and channels called a river delta is formed in a fan pattern, with many mouths emptying into the South China Sea. This is the Mekong's *Cuu Long*, or Nine Dragons. More than 1,000 miles (1,609 km) of canals crisscross the delta. With its roaring head in the mountains and its tail swishing in the South China Sea, the Nine Dragons mark the mouths of the Mekong River.

Water Puppets

Vietnamese *roi nuoc*, or water puppets, is a unique form of entertainment along the Mekong. The stage is a small pond of water, while the audience watches from the shore.

Thousands of years ago, the Mekong River started to build the delta by depositing sediments on the seafloor. Gradually, the land rose up from the sea. The yearly flooding of the Mekong River added river silt, creating the rich soil that produces the bountiful rice harvests of the Mekong Delta. The Vietnamese harvest two or three crops of rice each year from these fertile lands.

Ho Chi Minh City, once named Saigon, lies between the Mekong River Delta and the South China Sea. Ho Chi Minh City is the largest city in Vietnam and the nation's industrial and commercial center. The city is named for the Vietnamese leader who declared the country independent from France in 1945. When the Geneva Peace Conference of 1954 divided the country into two separate nations, Ho Chi Minh ruled the north while a French- and U.S.-backed government ruled the south.

Floating Markets

Many Vietnamese in the south live on boats near the rice fields or in city harbors. They buy produce from the Mekong Delta, which is sold in floating markets. Rice, vegetables, fruits, and fish nourished by the waters of the Mekong are sold from boats. The river even supports floating restaurants and gas stations for motor-powered boats.

The Mekong Delta was the scene of the heaviest warfare and bombing by U.S. forces during the Vietnam War (1955–1975). Thousands of tons of bombs were dropped on

A woman walks through an area that had been bombed with napalm.

Vietnam, Cambodia, and Laos in the 1960s and 1970s. Chemical **defoliants** stripped the leaves from trees along the Mekong, depriving the river of its green canopy and roots that held its banks. Toxic chemicals, including Agent Orange and napalm, polluted the waters of the river. Parts of the river were booby-trapped with mines.

After the Vietnam War ended in 1975, the need to rebuild southern Vietnam further taxed the Mekong and the forests around it. The demand for charcoal, fuel, wood, and timber exhausted the natural resources of the country. The new government's goal was to produce enough food for its people so it would not have to rely on other countries. For this, the Vietnamese depended upon the waters of the Mekong River and its annual deposit of silt that renewed the delta soils each year.

The Vietnamese developed new technologies and methods for raising fish, shrimp, and rice using the Mekong River waters. One new method of raising fish was in underwater farms. Houses were constructed on floats of empty metal drums and large underwater cages or pens were built under the floats to hold the fish.

The Vietnamese also developed a rice-shrimp farming culture in the Mekong Delta. Ditches are dug around fields and flooded with saltwater during the dry season. When the monsoon and its freshwater arrives, the salt is washed out of the fields into ditches along with the shrimp. By 1989, after combining new farming strategies such as these, Vietnam became self-sufficient in fish and the world's largest rice exporter after the United States and Thailand.

Can Tho, on the right bank of the Bassac or Lower River, is the unofficial capital of the Mekong Delta and the largest port on the Mekong. Ships arrive laden with machinery and fertilizers for the rebuilding of Vietnam's infrastructure and its agriculture. They leave carrying fish and agricultural products, nourished with the life-giving water of the Mekong River.

Timeline

2500 B.C.	First series of canals is built in Mekong Delta.
8th to 10th century	Thai people of South China migrate south following the Mekong.
1112–1152	Angkor Wat is built.
1172	Champa armies sack Angkor.
1182–1201	Jayavarman VII rules and builds the Bayon.
1520	King Phothisarat moves Lao capital to Vientiane on the Mekong.
1546	King Setthathirat has the That Luang Buddhist shrine built.
1560	Wat Xian Thong (Gold City Temple) is built.
1859	French colonial rule of Vietnam begins.
1945	Ho Chi Minh declares North Vietnam independent from France.
1953	Laos and Cambodia achieve independence.
1957	Mekong Development Committee is formed.
1961	President John F. Kennedy sends 16,000 U.S. troops to advise and train South Vietnamese.
1960s to 1970s	Bombs and chemical weapons are employed by U.S. troops in Vietnam, Cambodia, and Laos, which wreak havoc on the area's environment.
1969	The construction of Nam Ngum Dam begins in Laos.
1975	The Vietnam War ends.
1975–1979	Khmer Rouge in Cambodia creates the "killing fields."
1970s to 1980s	Vietnam develops rice-shrimp culture and fish farming.
1989	Vietnam becomes the world's third-largest exporter of rice.
1992	Angkor is established as a World Heritage site by UNESCO.

Glossary

Angkor—the capital and religious center of the Khmer empire in Kampuchea (Cambodia); means "city" in Sanskrit

Bayon—a large temple at Angkor Wat dedicated to Buddha, built by Jayavarman VII (1182-1201)

Champa—an ancient kingdom of southern Vietnam that flourished from the second century to the seventeenth century

confluence—the point where two rivers join

defoliant—a chemical used to strip trees of their leaves

delta—an area near the mouth of a river that consists of silt and sand deposits

fingerling—an immature fish, about the length of a finger

Golden Triangle—the area where Myanmar (Burma), Thailand and Laos meet; an opium-producing area controlled by rebel forces and private armies.

Green Revolution—a movement embraced by newly independent countries in Southeast Asia after World War II to help them become self-sufficient in rice

high-yielding rice—varieties of rice developed for the Green Revolution

hydroelectric energy—energy created by a turbine linked to an electric generator and powered by the force of water

Indochina—the name given to colonial states controlled by the French in Southeast Asia: Laos, Vietnam, and Cambodia

Khmer—a kingdom that existed from the sixth to the fifteenth centuries in today's Laos and Cambodia; its capital was located at Angkor

Khmer Rouge—a group led by Pol Pot, the creator of the infamous killing fields

Khone Falls—a series of cascades and drops along 7 miles (11 km) of the Mekong in Laos

Mekong Development Committee—a short term for the Committee for Coordination of Investigations in the lower Mekong Basin, founded in 1957

monsoon—a seasonal wind that changes direction every six months

mouth—the point at which a river empties into the sea

pirogue—a long canoe-like boat carved out of a single tree trunk

source—the point at which a river originates

To Find Out More

Books

Dramer, Kim. *People's Republic of China*. Danbury, CT: Children's Press, 1999.

——. *The Yellow River*. Danbury, CT: Franklin Watts, 2001.

Greenblatt, Miriam. *Cambodia*. Danbury, CT: Children's Press, 1996.

Mansfield, Stephen. *Laos*. Tarrytown, NY: Benchmark Books, 1998.

McNair, Sylvia. *Thailand*. Danbury, CT: Children's Press, 1998.

Organizations and Online Sites

Asia Society
http://www.asiasociety.org
This organization offers art exhibitions, films, programs for teachers and students, and information on Asia.

Ask Asia
http://www.askasia.org
This site provides a wealth of resources and cultural information on Asia. There is a special section for young people with fun activities and links.

International Rivers Network
1847 Berkeley Way
Berkeley, CA 94703
http://www.irn.org
This organization's mission is to protect river systems and to increase understanding, awareness, and respect for rivers. The organization's site has a section that features children's poetry and artwork on rivers.

United Nations Educational, Scientific, and Cultural Organization
http://www.unesco.org/whc/nwhc/pages/home/pages/homepage.htm
From this site, you can learn more about UNESCO's World Heritage Sites, such as Angkor.

Videos

Goddess Dancers of Cambodia: Classical Khmer Ballet. New York, NY: Media Services, Barnard College Library, 1987.

The JVA Video Anthology of World Music and Dance. Victor Company of Japan: Cambridge, MA. Distributed by Rounder Records, 1990.

Vietnam: A Television History. New York: Sony Corporation of America, 1983.

A Note on Sources

The fact that the Mekong River flows through six countries in Asia made writing this volume especially challenging. My goal was to make it clear to readers how the Mekong shaped the borders, histories, economies and cultures of each of these countries.

Like a river, a book needs to flow smoothly and steadily. Therefore, I first blocked out the order of the chapters in the book. For this task, I consulted a general encyclopedia entry. Then, I consulted more specialized books in the C.V. Starr East Asian Library at Columbia University as I wrote each chapter.

I was especially interested in making daily life on the Mekong come alive for the reader. In order to make the river and its people more immediate, I looked for books with vibrant color visuals that could be reproduced.

I included current, up-to-date sources so that I could address the future of the Mekong River as well as its rich and varied history. As ever, the waters of the Mekong will shape the course of history in Southeast Asia during the twenty-first century.

—Kim Dramer

Index

Numbers in *italics* indicate illustrations.

About the Author

Kim Dramer lives on the banks of the Hudson River. Here, she is completing her doctoral dissertation at Columbia University. She specializes in the art and archaeology of ancient China, the source of the Mekong River.

She is the author of numerous books for young adults, including *Enchantment of the World: China* and *Games People Play: China* for Children's Press and *The Yellow River* for the Watts Library series. Her future plans include a trip down the Mekong with her family.